The Fairy Dogfather

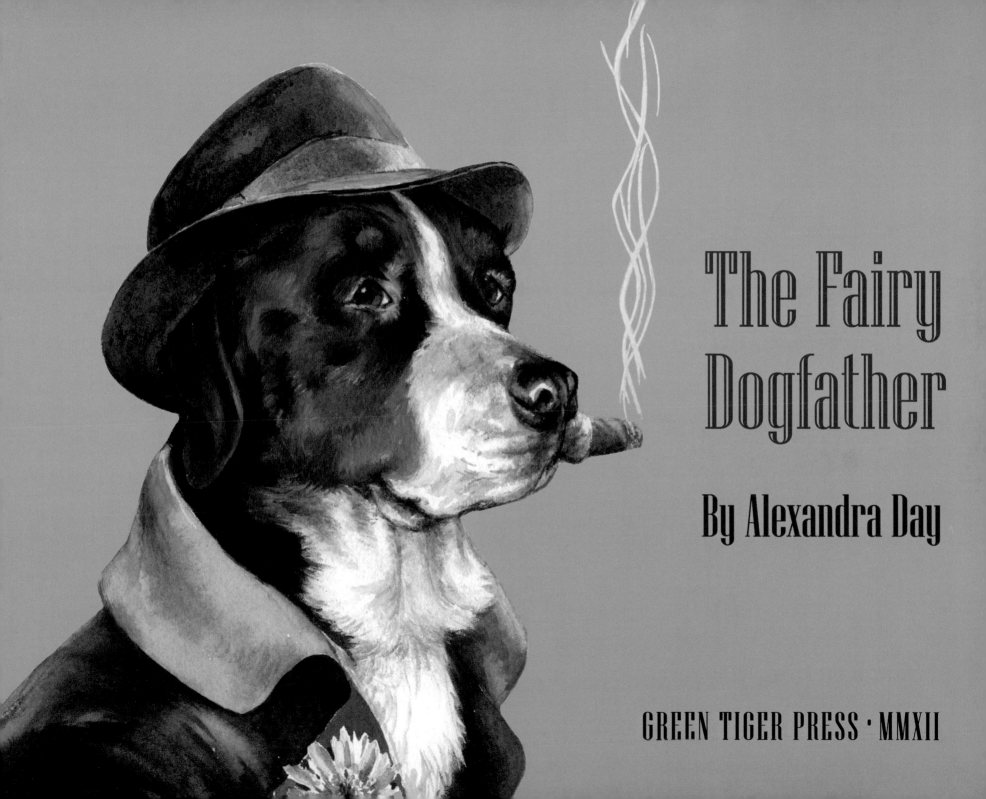

The Fairy Dogfather

By Alexandra Day

GREEN TIGER PRESS · MMXII

Thanks to Hector Leonidas Gerontakos and his parents Abigail Darling and Theodore Gerontakos.
Also, thanks to Lafcadio Darling and Gaber. — AD

GREEN TIGER PRESS
A division of Laughing Elephant

Copyright © 2012, Blue Lantern Publishing, Inc.
First printing. Printed in China. All Rights Reserved.

ISBN 978-1-59583-455-3

LAUGHING ELEPHANT
3645 Interlake Avenue North, Seattle WA   98103

LAUGHINGELEPHANT.COM

Library of Congress Cataloging-in-Publication Data

Day, Alexandra.
  The fairy dogfather / by Alexandra Day.
      p. cm.
  Summary: Hector, who has trouble differentiating between the letters "d" and "g", asks for a fairy godfather's
help in obtaining a special gift for his mother's birthday but the Fairy Dogfather who arrives instead is more
demanding than helpful.
  ISBN 978-1-59583-455-3
  [1. Dogs--Fiction. 2. Humorous stories.] I. Title.
  PZ7.D32915Fai 2012
  [E]--dc23
                           2011030525

Your writing is very good, Hector, but you must remember that the line on the 'g' goes down and the line on the 'd' goes up.

"Then, out of the bright, magical light stepped a beautiful lady. She said, 'I am your fairy godmother, Cinderella, come to grant your wish'..."

Mom, do boys get fairy godfathers?

I don't know, Hector. Ask your father. He used to be a boy.

I never heard of one, but it wouldn't hurt to put in a request.

That's a good idea.
I'll try it.

Is this or is this not your writing? I am your Fairy Dogfather, as you requested.

How did you get here?
How can a dog be magic?
Can you grant wishes?

You will discover that the manifestations of magic are many, and it doesn't do to underestimate dogs.

Where's the kitchen, kid? Being summoned always makes me hungry.

What's my mother going to say when she sees all this food missing?

Yes, I have a problem.
Tomorrow is my mother's birthday
and I don't have a present for her.

Have you failed to
formulate any ideas?

I wanted to buy her a beautiful plant with flowers. There's a red one at the garden store. I earned enough money, but...

What happened to it?

I put it carefully in my red box and then I don't know what happened to it. Can't you make it appear?

I observe that your mother does have
a strong predilection for the floral.
Ergo, your idea of a plant for a present
is excellent.

Have you developed any
new plan for obtaining
the necessary cash?

That's why I asked for you.

An excellent library of classics here, but I think for the present I'd like to peruse the paper.

Kindly depart and determine whether it's been delivered.

Can't you just wave your paw and get me a present? You are magic aren't you?

Where'd the vacuum cleaner come from? What's it for?

Yes, definitely a substantial disturbance in the upper atmosphere over the Caribbean. A judiciously timed departure is of the essence in successful travel.

I always use this superb machine in bad weather.

I could certainly cause a
gift to magically appear—
artistically wrapped, of
course. But in that case
it would be from me, not
from you, Hector. That
would hardly do the job,
would it?

Wake up, Hector.
Breakfast is ready.

My present money!

Thank you, Dogfather.

Darn that paperboy.
Where's my newspaper?

Can you take me to the
garden store this morning, Dad?